Archie and George and the Christmas Show

There are lots of Early Reader
stories you might enjoy.

Look at the back of the book or,
for a complete list, visit
www.orionchildrensbooks.co.uk

Archie and George and the Christmas Show

James Brown

Orion
Children's Books

ORION CHILDREN'S BOOKS

First published in Great Britain in 2016
by Hodder and Stoughton

1 3 5 7 9 10 8 6 4 2

A CIP catalogue record for this book
is available from the British Library.

ISBN 978 1 4440 1531 7

Printed and bound in China

The paper and board used in this book are from well-managed forests
and other responsible sources.

Orion Children's Books
An imprint of
Hachette Children's Group
Part of Hodder and Stoughton

Carmelite House
50 Victoria Embankment
London EC4Y 0DZ

An Hachette UK Company
www.hachette.co.uk

www.orionchildrensbooks.co.uk

For Christopher (my identical twin brother) and for his twins, Lucas and Rosanna – J.B.

Contents

Chapter One

This is Archie.

And this is George.

There is one easy way to tell them apart. George has a bit of hair that sticks up at the back of his head.

But just because they look similar does not mean they like the same things. Archie and George are very different.

Archie likes hot weather and playing outside.

George likes cold weather
and being inside with
a good book.

George likes Christmas.
He loves it when the shop
windows flash and flicker.

Archie does not like Christmas
shopping one bit. He hates
hearing the same songs over
and over.

"Why don't you like Christmas songs?" George asked one day at the supermarket.

"Because you sing them all the time!" Archie laughed

There was no way Archie would ever sing. Not even in front of George.

Chapter Two

It was nearly Christmas and the classroom was covered with snowmen and snowflakes.

"Come and sit on the carpet,"
Mrs Thomas said. "I have some
exciting news for you."

Archie and George looked at
each other and smiled.

"Next week," Mrs Thomas said, "we start rehearsing for the Christmas show! It's going to be a big talent show with acting, dancing and singing! Won't that be fun?"

There was a buzz of
excitement.

Archie groaned. He hated standing up in front of people.

How am I going to get out of this one? he thought.

"Home time," Mrs Thomas called. "And remember, everyone takes part in the Christmas show!"

Chapter Three

After school it was already
getting dark.

"I can't act. I can't dance. And I can't sing," Archie moaned.

Mum smiled. "It sounds like fun."

"I can't wait," George said.

George loved the limelight.
His favourite TV programmes
were talent shows. He'd sing
along and dance around the
living room.

"Maybe you could do your football tricks," Mum said to Archie.

"Maybe." Archie hadn't thought of that.

He could do keepy-uppies and balance the ball on his head.

But what if he dropped the ball? In front of all of his friends!

George sang all the way home.

Chapter Four

The next day at school, Mrs Thomas was standing on the stage. "Who would like to show us their talent?"

Lucy and Freya's hands shot up. They had made up their own dance routine.

Mo did some elf magic with Hammy, the school hamster.

Seth juggled with four
Christmas crackers.

Anais acted out a scene as
a snowflake.

"What a splendid start,"
Mrs Thomas said. "Next up is
Archie! You've brought your
football along. Show us what
you can do."

Archie went red. His cheeks were on fire.

"Mrs Thomas," George said, "I'd like to sing next, please."

Mrs Thomas nodded and Archie breathed a big sigh of relief. Thank you, he mouthed to George.

When George sang everyone
cheered.

Archie smiled from ear to ear.
George sang like a star.

Chapter Five

After school Mrs Thomas gave
Dad a piece of paper and a CD.

"This is a duet called 'Christmas Star'. We'd like Archie and George to sing it together. What do you think, boys?"

Archie and George were shocked.

"They'd love to," Dad said.

George ran home to listen
to the CD.

"This song's great!" he shouted, jumping up and down on the sofa with their sister Maddy.

"It's so catchy," she agreed.

Soon George could sing
without the words in front of
him.

Mum and Dad joined in too.

If only I could be as brave as George, Archie thought.

Maddy came over and sat next to Archie.

"Grandma and Grandad would love to see you sing on stage with George. Why don't you surprise them?"

George ran over. "We could practise together!"

Grandma and Grandad would
be surprised, Archie thought.
"Okay," he agreed.

Later that night, as he got ready for bed, Archie found himself singing into his toothbrush, just like George.

Chapter Six

In no time at all it was the big day.

Archie couldn't eat his breakfast. His tummy was full of butterflies.

"It'll be alright," Maddy said.
"Just pretend you're singing to
me."

Archie smiled. I can do this,
he thought. I can do this.

Archie and George went to get changed into their star costumes.

As they stood in front of the mirror it was hard to tell who was who.

"We look so silly," said George.

"No, you look like little stars!"
Mrs Thomas said. "Time to
shine, boys!"

Archie laughed. Maybe this
isn't so bad after all, he thought.

Suddenly it was their turn.
Archie stepped up to the stage.
His palms went cold and
sweaty and his knees felt
wobbly.

But when the tune to
'Christmas Star' started, Archie
saw Maddy beaming up at him.

Archie took a deep breath
and sang.

He was word perfect.
George was too.

As the class bowed, Maddy
jumped up, cheering and clapping.

Soon everyone in the
audience was doing the same.

After the show, George came over to Archie. "You were great," he said, smiling. "In fact, you were almost as good as me!"

And look out for more winter stories...

Find yourself **A Friend For Christmas** with Buddy the dog.

Or join the Weirdibeasts for their **Weird Snowy Day!**